THE
ELVES
AND THE
SHOEMAKER

Barefoot Books Inc.
41 Schermerhorn Street, Suite 145
Brooklyn, New York
NY 11201-4845

This book has been printed on 100% acid-free paper

Graphic design by Jennie Hoare
Color reproduction by Grafiscan, Verona
Printed and bound in Singapore by Tien Wah Press (Pte) Ltd

ISBN 1 901223 69 8

1 3 5 7 9 8 6 4 2

THE ELVES AND THE SHOEMAKER

THE BROTHERS GRIMM

ILLUSTRATED BY
MARGARET WALTY

BAREFOOT BOOKS

LONG AGO, a young shoemaker and his wife lived together in a beautiful city. The shoemaker worked hard all day and was very honest with all of his customers; but no matter how many shoes he made, he could not earn enough money for him and his wife to live upon. Finally, the day came when all that he had left in his workshop was one small piece of leather.

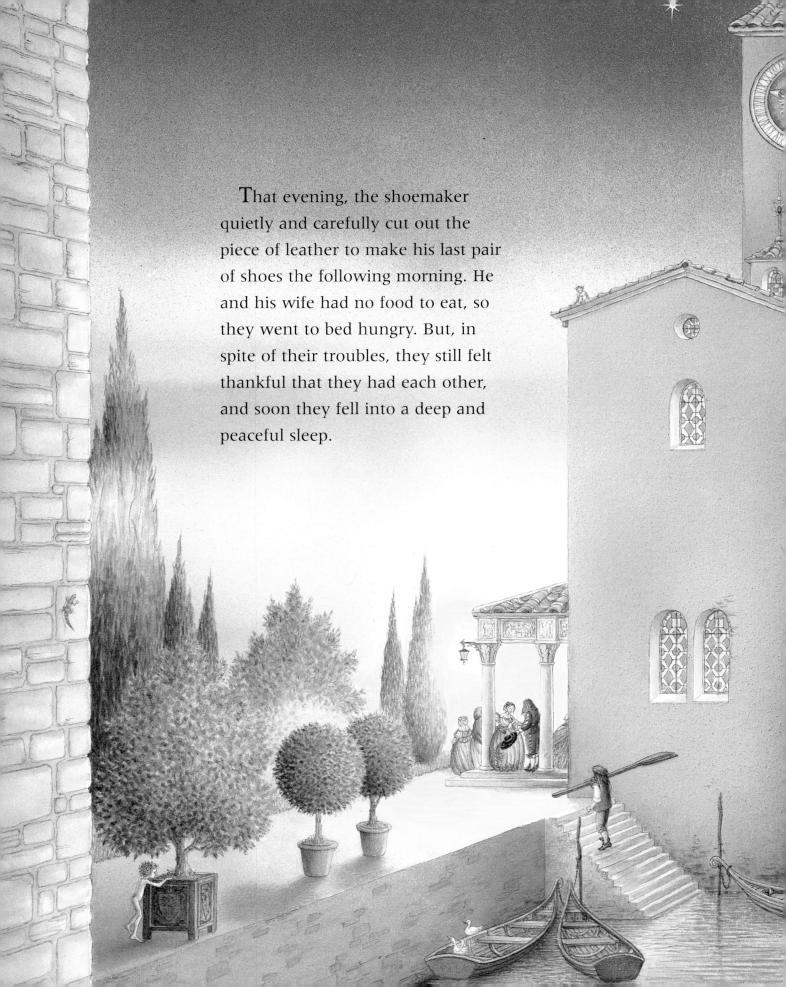

That evening, the shoemaker
quietly and carefully cut out the
piece of leather to make his last pair
of shoes the following morning. He
and his wife had no food to eat, so
they went to bed hungry. But, in
spite of their troubles, they still felt
thankful that they had each other,
and soon they fell into a deep and
peaceful sleep.

The next morning, the shoemaker and his wife woke up early. Without wasting a moment, the shoemaker went downstairs to do his work. To his astonishment, there on his worktable stood a fine pair of shoes, ready made!

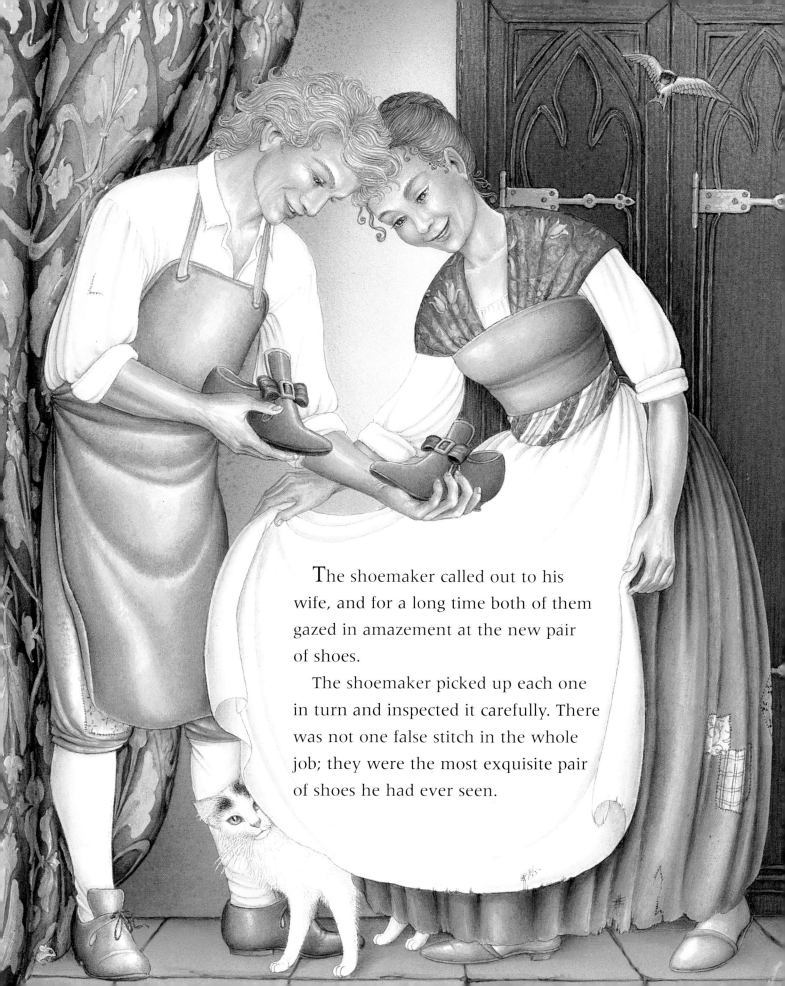

The shoemaker called out to his
wife, and for a long time both of them
gazed in amazement at the new pair
of shoes.

The shoemaker picked up each one
in turn and inspected it carefully. There
was not one false stitch in the whole
job; they were the most exquisite pair
of shoes he had ever seen.

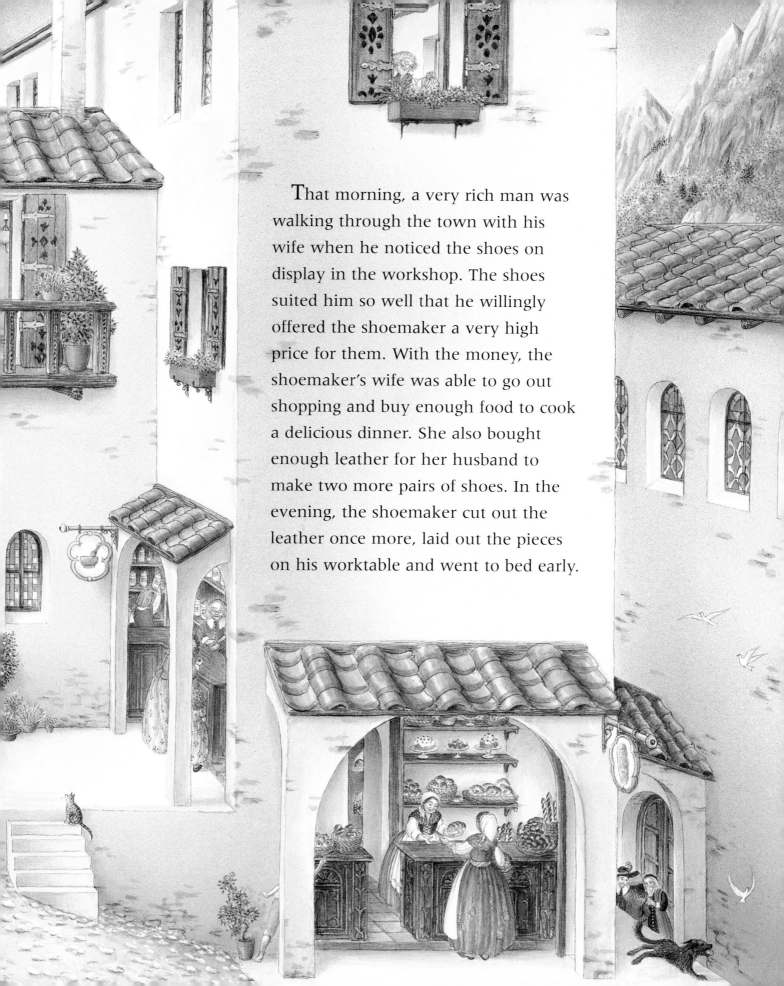

That morning, a very rich man was walking through the town with his wife when he noticed the shoes on display in the workshop. The shoes suited him so well that he willingly offered the shoemaker a very high price for them. With the money, the shoemaker's wife was able to go out shopping and buy enough food to cook a delicious dinner. She also bought enough leather for her husband to make two more pairs of shoes. In the evening, the shoemaker cut out the leather once more, laid out the pieces on his worktable and went to bed early.

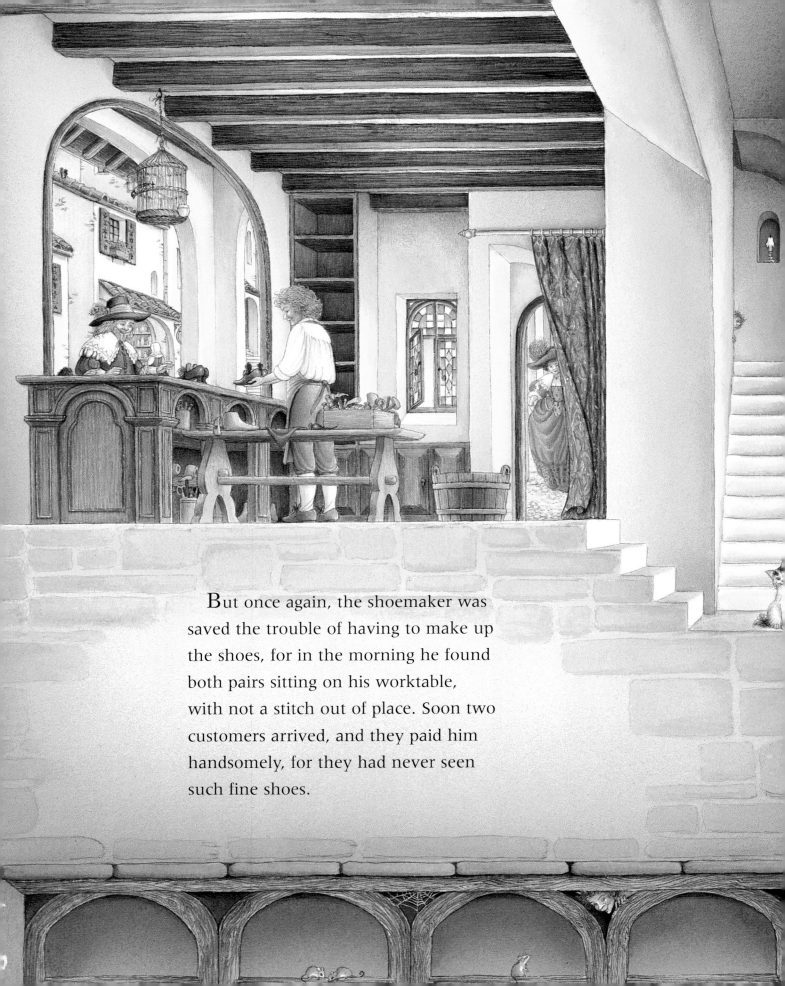

But once again, the shoemaker was
saved the trouble of having to make up
the shoes, for in the morning he found
both pairs sitting on his worktable,
with not a stitch out of place. Soon two
customers arrived, and they paid him
handsomely, for they had never seen
such fine shoes.

Now the shoemaker's wife could buy enough food to cook dinner and enough leather for four new pairs of shoes.

After the couple had eaten the shoemaker cut out the leather again and left it on his worktable. The same thing happened as had happened before: during the night, the leather that had been laid out in the evening was made into four perfect pairs of shoes.

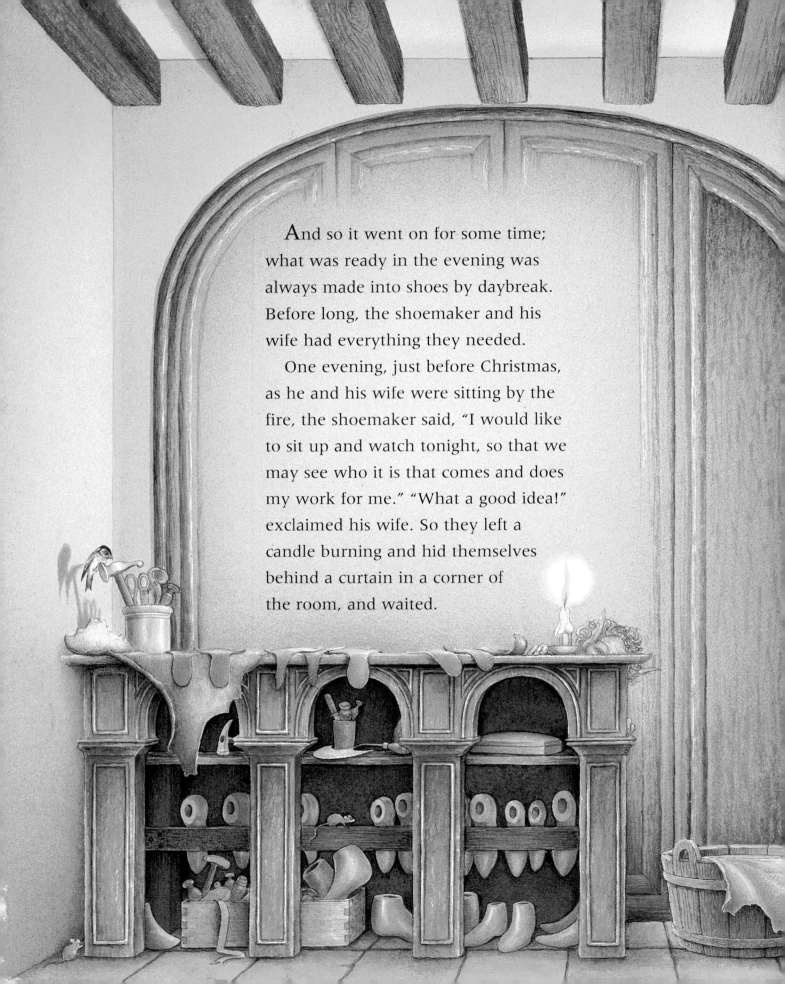

And so it went on for some time; what was ready in the evening was always made into shoes by daybreak. Before long, the shoemaker and his wife had everything they needed.

One evening, just before Christmas, as he and his wife were sitting by the fire, the shoemaker said, "I would like to sit up and watch tonight, so that we may see who it is that comes and does my work for me." "What a good idea!" exclaimed his wife. So they left a candle burning and hid themselves behind a curtain in a corner of the room, and waited.

As soon as the town clock struck midnight, in came two little elves, quite naked. They sat themselves down on the shoemaker's table, took up all the leather that was cut out, and set to work. They stitched and rapped and hammered and tapped faster than anyone the shoemaker had ever seen.

Within a few minutes the job was done, and a neat row of shoes stood ready for use upon the table. Then the two elves scurried away, as quickly and mysteriously as they had come.

While the couple were out walking together the next evening, the shoe-maker's wife stopped outside a draper's shop and said, "Those little elves have made us rich, and we ought to be thankful to them and do them a good turn if we can. I was quite sorry to see them going around with no clothes to keep them warm. Listen, I have an idea. I shall buy some scraps of fabric at this shop and make each of them a linen shirt, a silk waistcoat, and a velvet coat and pair of trousers into the bargain. You can make each of them a little pair of shoes."

This idea pleased the shoemaker
very much. So whenever they had a
free moment, he and his wife worked
on the elves' new outfits. At last,
everything was ready. That evening,
the couple laid the clothes out neatly
on the table, instead of the usual
pieces of leather. Then they lit a small
candle and hid themselves once more
behind the curtain.

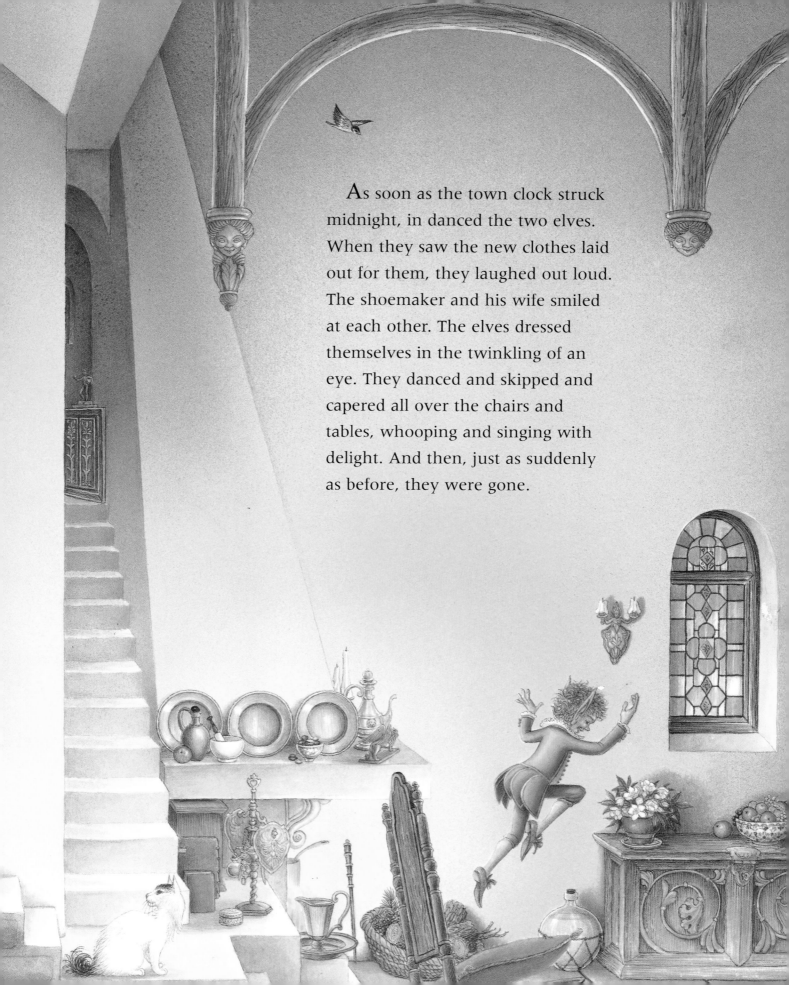

As soon as the town clock struck midnight, in danced the two elves. When they saw the new clothes laid out for them, they laughed out loud. The shoemaker and his wife smiled at each other. The elves dressed themselves in the twinkling of an eye. They danced and skipped and capered all over the chairs and tables, whooping and singing with delight. And then, just as suddenly as before, they were gone.

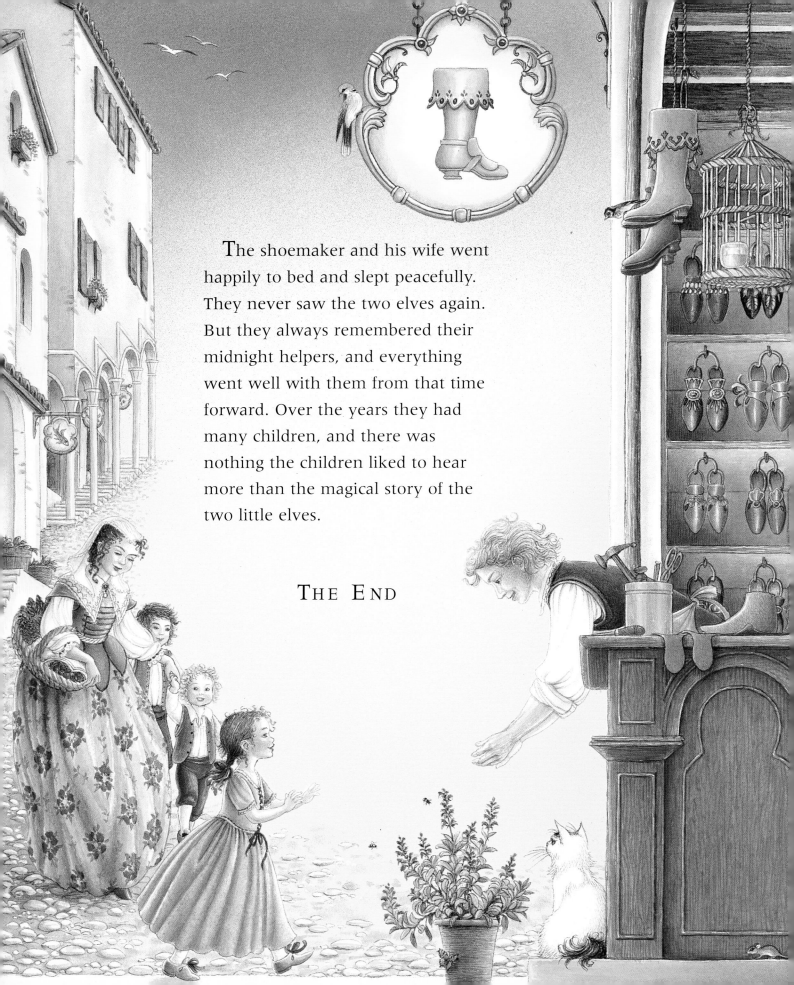

The shoemaker and his wife went
happily to bed and slept peacefully.
They never saw the two elves again.
But they always remembered their
midnight helpers, and everything
went well with them from that time
forward. Over the years they had
many children, and there was
nothing the children liked to hear
more than the magical story of the
two little elves.

THE END

BAREFOOT BOOKS publishes high-quality picture books for children of all ages and specializes in the work of artists and writers from many cultures. If you have enjoyed this book and would like to receive a copy of our current catalog, please write to our New York office:
41 Schermerhorn Street, Suite 145, Brooklyn, New York, NY 11201-4845
email: sales@barefoot-books.com website: www.barefoot-books.com